A Note from Michelle about
My Awesome Holiday Friendship Book

Hi! I'm Michelle Tanner. I'm nine years old. I love holidays, don't you? Christmas, the Fourth of July, Halloween—they're so much fun, especially when I can spend them with my friends!

My Awesome Holiday Friendship Book has awesome ideas for holiday parties—invitations, snacks, games, and decorations—everything you need to know to throw a party that will make your friends flip!

One of my favorite parties is the Backward April Fool's Day Party. Everyone has to wear their clothes backward, play games backward, and eat their dessert first. It's tons of *nuf*. (That's fun backward.)

I also have some great ideas for holiday presents you can make yourself—T-shirts, special stationery, hair bands, and more!

But you don't have to wait for a holiday to start having fun with your friends. Check out my boredom busters for lists ·of things to do any day of the year. Or try one of my quick quizzes to find out how much you know about your friends and how much your friends know about you!

Find out how you can make holidays—and every day—extra special with your friends.

FULL HOUSE™ MICHELLE novels

The Great Pet Project
The Super-Duper Sleepover Party
My Two Best Friends
Lucky, Lucky Day
The Ghost in My Closet
Ballet Surprise
Major League Trouble
My Fourth-Grade Mess
Bunk 3, Teddy and Me
My Best Friend Is a Movie Star! (Super Special)
The Big Turkey Escape
The Substitute Teacher
Calling All Planets
I've Got a Secret
How to Be Cool
The Not-So-Great Outdoors
My Ho-Ho-Horrible Christmas

Activity Book
My Awesome Holiday Friendship Book

Available from MINSTREL Books

FULL HOUSE™
Michelle

My Awesome Holiday
Friendship Book

Linda Williams Aber

A Parachute Press Book

Published by POCKET BOOKS
New York   London   Toronto   Sydney   Tokyo   Singapore

A MINSTREL PAPERBACK *Original*

A Minstrel Book published by
POCKET BOOKS, a division of Simon & Schuster Inc.
1230 Avenue of the Americas, New York, NY 10020

A PARACHUTE PRESS BOOK

READING   Copyright © and ™ 1997 by Warner Bros.

FULL HOUSE, characters, names and all related indicia are trademarks of Warner Bros. © 1997.

ISBN: 0-671-00840-4

First Minstrel Books printing December 1997

10 9 8 7 6 5 4 3 2 1

A MINSTREL BOOK and colophon are registered trademarks of Simon & Schuster Inc.

Cover photo by Schultz Photography

Printed in the U.S.A.

Contents

My Awesome Holiday
Friendship Book

Introduction

Holiday Greetings
from Michelle to You!

Hi! I'm Michelle Tanner. I'm nine years old. And I think holidays are the best times for making new friends. Friends make holidays and every day even more special.

Now I've told you my name. What's yours?

My name is _____.

(Write your name in this space.)

That's the way I begin most of my new friendships. When I see someone who looks friendly, I say, "Hi." I introduce myself and ask the person's name. Sometimes we can tell right away that we will like each other. Then we talk some more. Other times it takes a while to get to know a person. And sometimes I have to be the first one to say "Hi!" again and again each time we see each other.

Making friends isn't always easy. But it's always worth the effort when a new friend becomes a best friend.

Everywhere I go I find new friends. I meet friends at my ballet class, in the lunchroom at school, in after-school groups, on my soccer and baseball teams, and at holiday events. I even meet them right in my own neighborhood.

Where do you meet new friends?

I meet new friends _____

_____

_____

_____

_____

_____

_____.

My awesome holiday friendship book will give you lots of great ideas on how to fill your holidays and special days with new friends. And there's tons of fun stuff to do with those new friends once you meet them!

Making Happy Holiday Friends— Don't Be Shy, Just Say "Hi!"

Why not celebrate your next holiday with a new friend? What? You say you're too shy to make new friends? You get nervous and jittery inside when you meet someone new? Believe it or not, you're not the only one who feels shy when it comes to making friends. A lot of people feel the same way. But you can make this holiday a day to remember. Say "good-bye" to being shy! Here are some tips to get you started:

1. Smile! Even if you feel too shy to say "Hi!" you can break the ice with a warm smile. When the other person sees you being friendly, you'll get a smile back. That's a real winning beginning!

2. Be yourself! Don't try to act the way you think the other person wants you to act. Be the way you are with your own family—relaxed, talkative, friendly. Remember, the person you are meeting may be feeling nervous too. If you act relaxed, you'll help the other person feel relaxed.

3. If you have trouble talking about yourself—don't! That's right. Ask questions and let the other person do the talking. Show that you are interested in what he or she is doing, wearing, reading, or listening to. Your simple question could get a whole conversation going.

4. Give an honest compliment. Look for one thing you find interesting about the other person. Then say what you think. Do you like her new sweater? Is his key-chain collection really cool? Say so! You'll make the other person feel good. People like people who make them feel good about themselves.

Guess Who's New? You!

Uh-oh. The kid who's new is you! In the neighborhood. At school. At camp. On the team. Feeling a little uncomfortable? Have no fear, Michelle is here. Try out these easy icebreakers anywhere you're the newcomer. Pretty soon you'll feel welcomed.

1. Ask for directions—even if you know where you're going.

2. Ask what time it is—even if you already know.

3. Wear and carry items with your name printed on them. A T-shirt, a pencil case, a book bag, and anything else that is personalized will let kids, teachers, and coaches learn your name fast.

4. Do something interesting. If you're too shy to make the first move toward other people, let them make the first move toward you. Look up at the sky as though you see something fascinating. Sit under a tree with a sketch pad and draw. Bounce a ball under your leg until you break your own record. Sooner or later someone is sure to be curious and will ask what you're looking at or doing.

5. Be a helper. Share your terrific talents. Offer to help with holiday gift-wrapping, holiday shopping, hair braiding, a science fair project, batting practice, or learning a new piano piece. Whatever you're good at could get you in good with others!

To Have a Friend, Be a Friend

You've made a new friend. Now what can you do to make that new friend a good friend? Take a tip from me: Be a good friend and you'll have good friends. Here's how!

1. Share. Sharing means more than just splitting a candy bar. It means sharing your time, sharing your feelings, and sharing your good news and bad news. Holiday time is the perfect sharing time.

2. Talk. The thing that makes good friends great friends is talking. Talk about school. Talk about home. Talk about your plans for the holidays. Or just talk about how great it is to be friends. Talking is the best way to let your friend know more about who you are.

3. Listen. Being a good listener is one of the most important things a good friend can be. Give your friend a chance to talk while you just listen. Don't interrupt. Don't change the subject. Don't yawn (or at least cover your mouth if you do!). Listening is the best way you can learn more about your friend.

4. Care. Caring about a friend is the most rewarding part of a friendship. It makes you feel good to show that you care when your friend is sick or sad, happy or mad. When you show that you care, your friend will care about you too.

5. Call. When you are thinking about your friend—call! When something funny happens that you know would make your friend laugh—call! When you need help, advice, or an opinion—call! Calling your friend is a great way to show that you are a good friend. And be sure to be the first to call to say "Happy holidays!"

6. Write. Going away for the holidays? Don't forget to write to your friend. Even if you know you'll be back before your postcard or letter reaches your friend, write and send it. It's fun to get mail, especially from a good friend like you!

7. Remember. Remembering important events in your friend's life shows how valuable your friend is to you. Of course you'll always remember your friend's birthday. But there are other important events to think of too. Remember to ask how the piano recital went. Remember to ask how Grandmother is feeling. Remember to ask who won the game, how the weekend was, and when you two can get together again. Remembering to remember is thoughtful, caring, and very friendly.

Argument Enders

Being fair and showing respect and consideration for each other is the best way for friends to get along. But even the best of friends argue sometimes. There's nothing good about an argument except for one thing—ending it. How do you end a fight when you're so mad you can't even think straight? My "Argument Enders" will turn the frowns upside down!

1. Say "I'm sorry." Saying you're sorry can be hard. Really hard. But it's a great way to end a fight. And I bet if you say it this time, your friend will say it next time.

2. Flip a coin. Don't stand there arguing. Can't decide who should do something—you or your friend? Let a penny decide for you. The one who wins the flip wins the decision. The one who loses the flip wins the coin!

3. Write a note. Try wrapping a note around a piece of candy or gum. Write something simple such as: "Friends Forever!" Who can resist such a sweet message?

4. Find a photo. When you argue with a friend, you can forget that you ever had fun together.

Quick! Find a photo that shows the two of you smiling. Hand it to your friend. Then talk about what it was that made you smile when that picture was taken.

5. Call a Time-out. Don't go away mad. But do go away from each other for a few minutes. Sit in separate rooms and do nothing. Pretty soon you'll miss each other's company. You'll find it doesn't matter who was right or who was wrong. What matters is that friends belong together.

6. Make a Peace Offering. When friendship means everything, a special present is a wonderful way to make peace. What could be more special than a thoughtful gift?

2

Me, Myself, and I

What do you want new friends to know about you? Here's the place and the space to tell all. Fill in the pages in this chapter. Then, when you meet new friends, show them this chapter as an easy introduction to the one and only YOU!

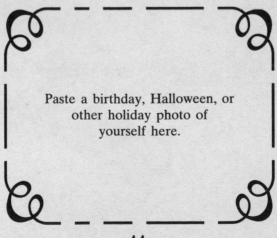

Paste a birthday, Halloween, or
other holiday photo of
yourself here.

This picture shows how I looked

on _____.

When this picture was taken I was _____ years

old. My next birthday is _____ _____,
(month)   (day)

19_____. As of that day I will be _____
(year)

years old.

My friends call me _____.
(Write your nickname here.)

I am _____ tall. My eyes are _____ .
(height)   (color)

My hair is _____.
(color)

12

More about Me

Three words that describe my personality are:

_____,

_____,

and _____.

Last year for Halloween I dressed up as _____

_____.

For my birthday last year I _____

_____.

For my birthday this year I will _____

_____.

My three favorite holiday gifts were:

1. _____,

2. _____,

3. _____.

I don't want to brag, *but* it's been said that I have:

❑ a great smile   ❑ a fabulous personality
❑ a cute giggle   ❑ a brain Einstein would
❑ talent galore   envy

13

- ❏ star athletic ability
- ❏ freckles that would make a leopard jealous
- ❏ a heart as big as all outdoors

Other good things about me (adorable dimples, piano-player fingers, great sense of humor, etc.):

_____

_____

_____

_____

_____

_____

_____

_____

_____

_____

_____

_____

_____

The Best Holiday Times Just Between Best Friends

My best best friend is _____

_____.

Over the holidays my best friend and I got together _____ times.

Our favorite thing to do together is _____

_____.

The best thing about my best friend is _____

_____

_____.

We exchanged gifts. I gave my best friend _____

_____.

My best friend gave me _____

_____.

The best thing about my best friend and me together is _____

_____

_____.

We get along so well because we both like _____

_____

_____ .

My other close friends are _____

_____

_____ .

If I could become better friends with someone, it
would be _____

because _____ .

Happiest Holiday Celebration Faces

Paste a picture of a friend here.

_____

(friend's name)

Paste a picture of a friend here.

_____

(friend's name)

Paste a picture of a friend here.

_____

(friend's name)

18

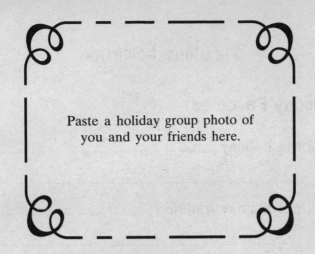

Paste a holiday group photo of
you and your friends here.

Friends' names from left to right: _____
_____

Fabulous Favorites

Holiday Favorites

Favorite holiday _____

_____

Favorite holiday tradition _____

_____

Favorite holiday activity _____

_____

Favorite holiday food _____

Favorite holiday song _____

_____

Favorite holiday outfit _____

_____

Favorite holiday party _____

Favorite holiday television special _____

_____

Everyday Favorites

Favorite school friend _____

_____

Favorite home friend _____

_____

Favorite thing about school _____

_____

Favorite thing about home _____

_____

Favorite Funniests

The funniest movie I ever saw was _____

_____.

The funniest book I ever read was _____

_____.

The funniest television show is _____

_____.

The funniest cartoon character is _____

_____.

The funniest joke I know is _____

_____.

The funniest friend I have is _____.

Favorite All-Time Favorites

Favorite color _____

Favorite song _____

Favorite movie _____

Favorite food _____

Favorite drink _____

Favorite snack _____

Favorite outfit _____

Favorite sport _____

Favorite kind of music _____

Favorite video _____

Favorite flavor _____

Favorite book _____

Favorite animal _____

Favorite hairstyle _____

Favorite collection _____

Favorite team _____

Favorite music group _____

Favorite computer game _____

3

Michelle's Quick Friendship Quizzes

Looking for a true test of friendship? I have plenty of them! My Quick Friendship Quizzes are as tried and true as friendship quizzes can be. Each one will tell you something different about you, your friends, and your friendships.

Take these quick quizzes with your friend in mind. Then let your friend take the test with you in mind. Get a pencil and a separate piece of paper so you can use the tests over and over again. Fill in your answers. Then check your score at the end of each test. Compare your answers with your friend's answers. My quizzes are a fun way to find out if your friendships are in ship shape!

23

Quick Quiz #1
How Well Do You
Know Your Friend?

Holiday gift-giving is easy when you know a lot about the person for whom you are buying the gift. Take this test and find out how well you know your friend.

1. What color are your friend's eyes? _____

2. How old will your friend be on his or her next birthday? _____

3. If the television set broke, what show would your friend miss most? _____

_____

4. Your friend would rather eat dirt than eat ___

_____.

5. If wishes came true, your friend's first wish would be _____

_____.

6. Your friend's favorite subject in school is ___

_____.

7. One famous person your friend would love to meet is _____.

8. Your friend's favorite snack is _____

_____

9. On a holiday your friend likes to _____

_____.

10. The happiest day in your friend's life was ___

_____

_____.

Michelle's Score Box

Give yourself two (2) points for every answer that is absolutely right. Give yourself one (1) point for each answer that is half right or sort of right, according to your friend. Give yourself zero (0) points for answers that are as wrong as wrong can be. Add up your points, then look below to find out how well you know your friend.

14–20 points: Congratulations! You know your friend so well, you could be twins! You two have shared a lot of feelings and thoughts. You're more than good friends, you're great friends!

25

7–13 points: Hmmm. You know your friend pretty well. But it seems you missed some of the important details a friend should know. Maybe a good sleepover would give you two time to catch up and get even closer!

0–6 points: Did you say you were friends? Maybe you meant you *want* to be friends. This test can help you learn more about each other. Take turns reading and answering the questions. At the end of the quiz you'll be on your way to having a good, strong friendship!

Quick Quiz #2
What Would You Do If?

1. You and your friend are at a birthday party together. There's one piece of cake left and you both want it. You:

a) Grab the last piece first and say, "You lose!"

b) Divide the cake in two equal pieces and share it.

c) Let your friend have it. You like your friend more than you like cake.

d) Let your friend have it, but then act mad for the rest of the party.

2. Your friend just got a really ugly haircut right before the biggest party of the year. You:

a) Point, laugh, and ask, "What happened? Did your head get stuck in the lawn mower?"

b) Don't say anything except to offer to lend your friend your favorite hat.

c) Cross your fingers behind your back and say, "It doesn't look that bad. And besides, it's what's inside that counts."

d) Say it looks nice, then call everyone you know to laugh about it behind your friend's back.

3. Your best friend is paying more attention to the new kid in class than to you. You feel jealous so you:

a) Accidentally on purpose bump into the new kid and make her drop her books.

b) Interrupt with a friendly "Hi!" and introduce yourself as your friend's best friend.

c) You ask your friend to introduce you to the new kid so you can all be friends.

d) Ignore your friend and the new kid.

4. You and your friend both tried out for the lead in the holiday play. You got the part! Your friend made the chorus with the rest of the class. You:

a) Tell your friend you'll let her help you put on your beautiful costume.

b) Explain nicely that everyone has a special talent, and acting just happens to be yours.

c) Say, "You were good too. You'll get it the next time!"

d) Tell your friend you'll have to get together after the play is over because you'll just be too busy with rehearsals now.

Michelle's Score Box

Give yourself two (2) points each time you chose the letter (a). Give five (5) points each time you chose the letter (b). Give ten (10) points each

28

time you chose the letter (c), and zero (0) points each time you chose the letter (d).

30–40 points: Congratulations! You are thoughtful, generous, and caring. You're the kind of friend I'd like to have—and I bet lots of other people feel the same way.

20–29 points: You are definitely a friend others would want to have and keep. You try to be thoughtful all the time. But be careful. Sometimes you get a little jealous. And sometimes your sense of humor might hurt the feelings of others.

9–19 points: Try spending a little more time thinking about how your friends are feeling. Read the questions again. Imagine it is your best friend taking the test instead of you. Which answers do you wish your friend would give? The type of friend you want to have is the type of friend you need to be. Give it your best. Good friends are worth the effort!

0–8 points: Oh, no! Could this really be your score? There must be some mistake. This score would mean that you aren't as nice as you think you are. But that can't be *you!* Can it? Take a break and then take the test again. When it comes to friendships, everyone deserves a second chance.

Quick Quiz #3
You Are a Good Good Friend.
True or False?

1. It's your friend's birthday. You remembered.
    ❏ True   ❏ False
2. Your friend was out sick today. You drop off the homework.
    ❏ True   ❏ False
3. You haven't heard from your friend all week. You pick up the phone and call.
    ❏ True   ❏ False
4. You're on vacation having a wonderful time. You write a postcard to your friend saying, "I miss you!"
    ❏ True   ❏ False
5. You're sitting with a group of friends at the lunch table. Your friend walks in and looks for you. You call out, "Over here! I saved you a seat!"
    ❏ True   ❏ False
6. You hear someone saying something mean about your friend. You interrupt and say, "Hey! That's my friend you're talking about!"
    ❏ True   ❏ False
7. Your friend just found out she's moving. You cry with her.
    ❏ True   ❏ False

8. Your friend doesn't understand the math. You offer to help.
    ❏ True   ❏ False
9. Your friend wants to talk about a personal problem with you. You listen.
    ❏ True   ❏ False
10. The whole group of kids is going ice skating. Your friend lost her wallet and asks you to help her look for it. If you do, you'll miss out on skating. You stay and help her look for the wallet.
    ❏ True   ❏ False

Michelle's Score Box

Give yourself two (2) points for every true answer and one (1) point for every false answer.

17–20 points: Congratulations! You are a true friend! You put others before yourself, and that's a sign of a good friend. You're a winner!

13–16 points: Not bad, but not great either. Have you thought of being a little more thoughtful? Friendship is like a reflection in the mirror: You get back what you put into it. Think about it.

10–12 points: Yikes! You aren't giving yourself a chance to feel how good good friendships can be! Remember: If you choose yourself over others too often, you'll find yourself by yourself more often!

Quick Quiz #4
What Do You Have in Common?
Dare to Compare!

FAVORITES

You   **Your Friend**

Color

_____   _____

Candy

_____   _____

Party game

_____   _____

Holiday movie

_____   _____

Holiday TV show

_____   _____

32

Ice cream

_____   _____

Vacation spot

_____   _____

Holiday activity

_____   _____

Holiday song

_____   _____

Michelle's Score Box

You may be surprised to find out that there is no score on this quick quiz. Nobody is wrong. Nobody is right. Everybody has the right to be different.

If you and your friends have diffcrent likes and dislikes, it really doesn't matter. All that matters is that you like each other!

Shhhhhh! It's a Secret!

It's no secret that secrets are fun to share and fun to keep. Of course, good friends know that keeping secrets secret is very important. So before you tell all, give your friend the "Super Secret-Keeping Test." Let the test results help you decide whether or not to share your secrets. And when you're ready to tell all to a friend, pass the secret along using Michelle's Holiday Secret Code Cards and Shhhhh! Super Secret Language.

Michelle's Super Secret-Keeping Test

Wait! The holidays are here and they're full of secrets and surprises! Will your secrets be safe with your friend? Will your friend's secrets be safe with you? Before you share secrets, take this test together. Find out just how good you are at keeping secrets secret. Answer the questions. Then check your score in Michelle's Score Box at the end of the test. Are you a Secret Keeper or a Secret Leaker? Find out now!

1. The best way for you to keep a secret is to

a) write it down on a piece of paper and keep it in a drawer.

b) put tape over your mouth so you won't be able to talk.

c) not tell anyone no matter what.

2. Out of the last two secrets told to you, you kept

a) none of them.

b) one of them.

c) two of them.

3. Best Friend #1 wants to tell you a secret about your Best Friend #2. You

a) listen to the secret. Then tell Best Friend #2 what you heard. After all, it's a secret about her!

b) tell best Friend #2 that you heard a secret about her. Then make a deal to tell her if she will lend you her new CD.

c) tell Best Friend #1 not to tell you. You'd rather not have to keep a secret about another friend.

4. You're walking past your big brother's bedroom. He's on the phone telling his friend how much he likes your best friend's older sister. You

a) stop and put your ear up to the door so you can hear more, then call your best friend as soon as your brother hangs up and tell her what you heard.

b) make noise so your brother will know you're out there.

c) keep on walking and don't listen.

5. In school you find a folded-up note labeled SECRET. You

a) read it out loud the next time you're called on to read something.

b) read it and then throw it away.

c) turn it in to the teacher without reading it.

6. You think secrets are

a) made to be shared . . . with the world.

b) made to be shared with a friend.

c) made to be kept to yourself.

Michelle's Score Box

Give yourself one point for each letter (a) you answered, two points for each letter (b), and three points for each letter (c). Add up your points and find what your score means.

6–9 points: Congratulations! When it comes to keeping secrets, your lips are sealed. You can be trusted with any secrets anytime. Secrets are safe with you. Consider yourself a genuine Secret Keeper!

10–13 points: Shhhhhh! Your friends shouldn't tell a secret to you unless they make you promise a hundred times that you won't tell no matter what. You want to keep secrets, but sometimes you just can't. You better work on your secret skills. Here's the first secret you should practice keeping: You can't keep a secret!

14–18 points: Blabber, blabber, blabber! With you around, nobody needs to watch TV to get the latest news or read the paper. You'll tell all! Sorry. Your secret is out: You are a Secret Leaker!

Michelle's Shhhh! Super Secret Language

Show-nay shear-hay shis-thay! (Now hear this!) Shis-thay shis-ay Shi-may-Shelle-chay's she-say-shet-cray shang-lay-shuage-ay (This is Michelle's secret language.) Do you get it? Learning my secret language is as easy as shie-pay (that's pie)! Just follow these simple rules.

In a one-syllable word beginning with a consonant, move the consonant to the very end of the word and add "ay." Then add the sound "sh" to the beginning of the word. So to say the word "Hi," here's what you do: SHi-hay. (Move the H to the end, add "ay," to the end, add SH to the beginning.)

In words with more than one syllable you treat each syllable like a separate word and follow the same rules. So the word "super" would be SHu-say (su) SHer-pay (per).

If a word starts with a vowel sound, like the word "ear," put the "SH" in front of the whole word and add the ay at the end (SHear-ay). Words that start with double consonants like "friend" get the SH sound added after the first two letters. The first two letters are moved to the end of the word and "ay" is added at the end. So friend would be "SHiend-fray."

Once you learn the language, you and your friends can talk or write notes in secret. Here are some commonly used words and phrases to help you get started.

Hello—SHell-hay-SHo-ay
Good-bye—SHood-gay-SHye-bay
Yes—SHes-yay
No—SHo-nay
Happy Birthday—SHappy-hay SHirth-bay-SHay-day
Merry Christmas—SHerry-may SHrist-cay-SHas-may
Trick-or-Treat—SHick-tray-SHor-ay-SHeat-tray
Be My Valentine—SHe-bay SHy-may SHal-vay-SHen-ay-SHine-tay
Friends forever!—SHiends-fray SHor-fay-SHev-ay-SHer-ay!

Michelle's Secret Code Cards

Want to give your friends a real holiday treat? Send them your holiday greetings in code! These Secret Code Cards make exchanging holiday greetings even more special.

Carefully cut out the Secret Code Cards. To make your Code Cards stronger, tape or glue them onto index cards. Using scissors, cut out the small rectangles on the cards. These will be your code windows. Both cards have the windows in the same places.

When you are ready to write your holiday note, place a Code Card over the piece of paper you are using for the note. Trace the border of the card. Then write your message in the code windows of the card.

When you are finished writing your message, lift the Code Card off the paper. Now write other letters before and after your message words. Your secret message will be "lost" in all the other letters.

Pass your note to your friend. Your friend will be able to read your message by placing the other Code Card over the paper. Your message will appear in the code windows.

Your holiday secrets will be safe thanks to my Secret Code Cards.

FULL HOUSE™ MICHELLE SECRET CODE CARDS

1. Cut out both cards.
2. Cut out all the rectangles.
3. Give one card to a friend. Keep the other one for yourself.
4. To write your secret note follow the directions on the previous page.

FULL HOUSE™ MICHELLE SECRET CODE CARD

FULL HOUSE™ MICHELLE SECRET CODE CARD

(CUT ALONG DOTTED LINE)

Things to Do When
There's Nothing to Do

Not every day is a holiday. Some days can be pretty boring. And what could be more boring than being bored? When I feel boredom creeping up on me, I know just what to do. I take out this handy list of boredom busters. As soon as I start reading the list, boredom disappears! It works for me and it can work for you too.

Indoor Boredom Busters

1. Make up a song about how bored you are. Or make up a new song for the upcoming holiday. Then call a friend and sing it.

2. Fix something that needs fixing.

3. Hunt for treasure in your own home. Lift sofa and chair cushions to find loose change. Look behind things that never get moved to find long-lost toys. Check the "junk" drawer and discover things you never knew were there.

4. Organize your collection—stickers, jewelry, baseball cards, or whatever. Then have a "swap meet" with a friend and trade stuff.

5. Invent a new holiday snack. Challenge a friend to a snack-invention contest. See who makes the best-tasting, most original snack. Make your snack a holiday tradition!

6. Create a hairstyle for your holiday party. Using water, mousse, or gel, come up with a new hairstyle without using scissors.

7. Play dress up with old clothes or fancy clothes from your own house.

8. Write secret Valentine notes, birthday surprise messages, or scary Halloween notes. Hide them all over the house—in sock drawers, kitchen cabinets, the hall closet, on the bathroom mirror, etc. Surprise everyone who finds them.

9. Make birthday cards for all your friends and family members.

10. Earn holiday spending money at home. Ask your parents to hire you to alphabetize the bookshelf; put loose photos into albums; clean a closet; polish silver; clean the bird cage or pet dishes.

11. Decorate your sneakers. Glue fake jewels on them, paint them with neon fabric paints, change the laces.

12. Watch a holiday special on television. Count the commercials. Count how many times the announcer uses the words "new," "improved," or "better."

13. Make a funny tape recording alone or with a friend. Record a fake commercial; record sound effects (your dad snoring, your mom laughing, your brother slamming the door, etc.).

14. Learn how to do something new—how to eat with chopsticks; how to fold fitted sheets; how to crack an egg without getting any shell in it; how to set the time on the VCR; how to rollerblade, ice-skate, or roller-skate; how to peel a carrot; how to stand on your head; how to blow the biggest bubble with bubble gum; how to do anything you don't know how to do but wish you did.

15. Play wastebasket basketball. Practice tossing a ball of paper into the can. Have a contest with a friend or try to beat your own record.

16. Test the post office. Write a holiday card and send it to yourself. Mail it and see how long it takes to get to you.

17. Build a pillow fort.

18. Color in the daily comics.

19. Make a rubber-band ball and have a bouncing contest with a friend.

20. Make a list of ten things to do indoors when there's nothing to do.

Outdoor Boredom Busters

1. Shovel snow on snowy days.

2. Have a snowperson- or snowanimal-making contest—make something other than a snowman for a change!

3. Track animal footprints in the snow.

4. Make snow ice cream sundaes. Use clean, fresh snow for ice cream and cover it with your favorite toppings.

5. Make snow angels. Lie down in freshly fallen snow. Spread your arms and legs out and bring them in close to your body again. Get up carefully and don't step in your angel outline. You can try this in wet sand at the beach too.

6. Hunt for four-leaf clovers for St. Patrick's Day.

7. Start the summer vacation off with a splash. Have a water-balloon fight with a friend.

8. Plan a vacation day garage sale. Sell your old toys, books, and puzzles. Use the money to treat yourself and your friends to an ice cream cone.

9. Go on a nature scavenger hunt. Each hunter takes along a paper bag. Look for a broken bird egg (on the ground only, not from a nest!), feathers, pretty stones, leaves, tree bark, and more.

10. Have a kite-flying contest. See whose kite flies highest.

11. Follow a neighborhood cat and see where it goes.

12. Float paper boats in puddles on rainy days.

13. Plan a bike trip. Pack a picnic and have a great day.

14. Sell lemonade in summer or hot chocolate in winter.

15. Wash the family car with a friend. Wear bathing suits just in case you get wet!

16. Plant a garden of berries to pick later.

17. Start a detective club. Have a meeting in a secret hiding place. Then get to work on your first case, finding something that is lost.

18. Make bird feeders out of pine cones covered with peanut butter. Give them as gifts to nature lovers.

19. Decorate an outdoor tree with lights, plastic toys, or anything you like. Do this any time of year.

20. Make a list of ten things to do outdoors when there's nothing to do.

Party Hardy

Holidays and special events become even more special when friends are included. Parties are the perfect way to make your friends part of the event. Don't wait for a birthday to celebrate. Any day is the right day for a party!

My favorite party ideas include a sleepover party, a costume party, a makeover party, a trading party, a treasure hunt party, and a camp-out party. Try one or try them all. But whatever you do, party hardy!

Michelle's Party Planning Tips

When it comes to parties, planning is everything! No matter which type of party you have, it's important to plan carefully. Here are Michelle's tips for perfect party planning.

1. Make up your guest list. Decide if you want to have a big party or a small party. If it's going to be a small party, try to choose guests you know will get along.

2. Send out invitations at least two weeks ahead of time. That way your friends will keep your party date open on their calendars. Invitations should include the date, time, place, what to wear, and your phone number for responses.

3. Plan your party activities well. Good parties have something going on all the time. Chapters 7 and 8 are full of games to play and things to make. Add some great food to the party, and it's sure to be a success!

4. Decorations add to the festive feeling of a party. Your decorations can be as simple as balloons or as fancy as crepe paper, confetti, and homemade wall hangings in the theme of the party.

5. Take all the help you can get. Let an adult or older sisters and brothers help fill out the invitations, decorate the party room, run the games, make the food, and *clean up!*

6. Have fun at your own party. Once your party is planned, you can join in the party fun with everyone.

7. Take lots of pictures!

New Year's Eve Jammin'
Pajama Party

Tell your friends to pack their overnight bags and get ready to ring in the new year at your house! This New Year's Eve Jammin' Pajama Party is a sleepover they'll flip over.

Jammin' Pajama Invitations

Making your own invitations is fun. For this invitation, draw a simple outline of a nightgown on colored construction paper. Write your party information on the nightgown.

It's a New Year's Eve Jammin' Pajama Party!

Wear your jams and come sleep over at _____ _____'s house!

Address: _____

Date: _____ Time: _____

R.S.V.P. _____

Bring a sleeping bag and get set to party all night!

Jammin' Pajama Party Setup

Pillows, pillows, and more pillows! Fill the Jammin' Pajama Party room with plenty of fluffy stuff. Throw pillows, bed pillows, and plenty of puffy stuffed animals set the mood for your special sleepover party. This is the Comfort Zone created especially for your Jammin' Pajama Party guests. You supply the pillows and plenty of horns and noisemakers to welcome the New Year in with a blast.

Food for a Jammin' Good Time

A pancakes and waffles supper is super! Set up a buffet table filled with plates of pancakes and waffles. Bowls of syrup, cinnamon, jam, and fruits tempt party guests to pile on the toppings. Serve it all with cold milk or a fruity sparkling punch made with two quarts of orange juice, one quart of ginger ale, and two pints of lemon or orange sherbet.

Howlin' House-to-House
Halloween Costume Party

A costume party! A costume party is great any day of the year. But it's a boo-tiful way to celebrate Halloween! Get all your ghoul-friends together for a howlin' good time. Start the fang-tastic fun at your house, then move on to the next house. Eat some sweet treats at your house. Do crafts at the next house. Watch a scary movie at the third house. It's a moving experience you'll all enjoy!

Boo-tiful Invitations

Draw an outline of a ghost on white paper. Write your party information on the ghost.

It's a House-to-House Howlin' Halloween Party! Wear your Halloween costume and come to

House #1, _____'s house.

Address: _____

Date: _____ Time: _____

The fun starts here. And moves on to House

#2, _____'s house, then to House

#3, _____'s house.

R.S.V.P. to _____.

A moving experience with food, crafts, and fun for all!

House #1: Frightful Food

I Scream Sundaes: Let your guests make their own ice cream creations. Set your party table with bowls of ice cream for each guest and plenty of tempting toppings such as chocolate, butterscotch, and marshmallow whip, chocolate chips, nuts, Gummi Bears, sprinkles, and candy corn. **Slime Time Punch:** Mix together one quart lemon-lime soda, two quarts grape juice, and two pints of lime sherbet.

House #2: Creepy Crafts

Move to the second house for some craft fun for everyone. Decorate small pumpkins or create creepy Halloween masks.

What you'll need for both crafts: small pumpkins, paints, paste, heavy colored construction paper, and decorative doodads such as sequins, feathers, macaroni, buttons, and yarn.

Supply a small pumpkin for each guest or a precut construction-paper face mask. Your guests will howl with laughter when they see each other's creations.

House #3: Welcome to Horror Show Time!

A VCR and an old black and white horror movie are all you need to get the ghouls shrieking. Turn out the lights, turn on the movie, and see who howls the loudest. Check your local video rental store for some of the classic horror movies. Then have a very scary time!

Lookin' Good Valentine's Day
Makeover Luncheon

New hairstyle, new face, new fashions! This Valentine's Day party idea is one my friends and I are always in the mood for. You and your friends will think this makeover party is a beautiful way to spend a day too.

Lookin' Good Invitations

In the center of a lacy doily, draw a girl's face. Use markers to color in eye shadow, lipstick, and blush. Write your party information on the other side of the face drawing.

Color in this face and come to a Lookin' Good Valentine's Day Makeover Luncheon!

Have a fashion-fun day at _____'s house!

Address: _____

Celebrate you! Bring yourself and a hairbrush! It's a beauty-up party on

Date: _____ Time: _____

R.S.V.P. _____

Lookin' Good Makeover Setup

This party room is a thing of beauty! In fact, it's filled with all the beauty supplies your guests need to start their makeovers. Set up four Lookin' Good Beauty Stations. A simple table with a mirror makes a perfect station. Make signs for each station: MAKEUP STATION; MANICURE STATION; HAIRSTYLE STATION; JUST-FOR-FUN STATION. At the makeup station, place eye shadows, lipsticks, blushes, mascara, Q-tips, tissues, and cold cream. At the manicure station supply several nail polishes, nail polish remover, nail tattoos, nail jewels, and cotton balls. At the hairstyle station supply barrettes, hair ribbons, scrunchies, hairbands, and butterfly clips. And at the just-for-fun station, supply stick-on earrings, fake tattoos, bracelets, necklaces, sunglasses, hats and scarves. Guests can take turns helping themselves and helping each other.

Lookin' Good Luncheon

A salad bar buffet is just the thing to serve at a Lookin' Good Luncheon. Guests take a plate and create their own super salads from the ingredients you've supplied: lettuce, tomatoes, cucumbers, carrots, celery, green pepper strips, bacon bits, croutons, and a selection of salad dressings. Serve it with soft drinks or flavored ice teas. Good tastes for the guests who are lookin' so good!

Fourth of July Treasure Hunt Party

Add a little mystery to the next Fourth of July picnic. Invite your friends to a Fourth of July Treasure Hunt Party! This outdoor picnic party will make your Fourth of July a memory you'll always treasure!

Treasure Hunt Invitations

Make your invitation look like a treasure chest. Write your party information on the chest.

It's a Fourth of July Treasure Hunt and Hike!

Come to the party at _____'s house.

Address: _____

Date: _____ Time: _____

R.S.V.P. _____

A treasure is waiting to be found by *you!*

Treasure Hunt Setup

First, pick a spot where the treasure will be hidden. This treasure hunt will also be a hike, so the clues should take the treasure hunters on a good long walk that finally leads back to your Fourth of July picnic place.

Every treasure hunt needs a treasure. Any box becomes a treasure chest when it's filled with something valuable. Fill your box with gold coins (foil-covered chocolate coins are perfect) or fistfuls of costume jewelry such as necklaces, pins, bracelets, and dangly earrings. Cover the box in gold foil wrapping paper and hide it in your picnic area.

Prepare clues that lead the treasure hunters to the next clue, the next clue, and the next, until finally the treasure may be found. The more clues you make, the longer the hunt will be. Here are some clue ideas to get you started.

Clue #1: Here's Clue #1,
Take ten steps to the right
And Clue #2 will be in sight!

Clue #2: You found this clue
But no treasure you see.
Look by a fire hydrant
For Clue #3.

Divide your party group into two teams, or send the hunters out individually. Tell each team or hunter to try to keep clue discoveries secret.

The one or ones who find the treasure chest keep what they find.

Treasure Hunt Picnic Lunch

Spread a big picnic blanket on the ground, or on a picnic table. Cold fried chicken, pasta salads, soft drinks, and platters of luncheon meats, spreads, and breads for sandwiches make a great picnic lunch for hungry treasure hunters. For dessert, hand out foil-covered gold coins and Popsicles.

More Hardy Parties from Michelle

For a party girl like me, there can never be too many parties. Here are some other party ideas that are sure to liven up your holidays, birthdays, and any special days. Any foods and drinks I told you about will work well for these parties too. Or simply serve the never-fail party pleasers, cake and ice cream.

Backward April Fool's Day Party

Everyone should act a little silly on April Fool's Day. That's why it's the perfect time for a Backward Party. No one is allowed to come unless they wear their clothes backward. When your friends arrive, serve them their dessert first. Then try playing your favorite games backward. In Backward Hide-and-Seek, for example, the person who is "it" hides—and everyone else looks for her. When someone finds the hidden person, she quietly hides with that person. Soon the whole party will be squeezed into one spot. The last one to join the group is the next "it."

Super Swap 'n' Shop Labor Day Party

Collectors, unite! You've worked long enough putting your collection together. Now put your collectors together. It's a party where collections can be displayed, compared, and traded. Tell your party guests to bring their collections to the greatest Swap 'n' Shop Labor Day Party ever held. Any collection will do—stickers, stuffed animals, postcards, erasers, key chains, stamps, coins, books, or whatever. You supply the Swap 'n' Shop snacks and drinks, and let the collection party provide the fun!

Camp-out-in-Winter-Break Party

Weather or not, a camp-out can always happen if you camp in! During your next school winter break, invite your friends over for a camp-out inside. Have them dress in their jeans and sneakers. Set up blanket tents and sleeping bags in the party room. Turn out all the lights. Hand out flashlights to everyone. Make a flashlight "campfire" in the middle of the room. Sit around the "campfire" and tell ghost stories, sing camp songs, and munch on some camp-out specials such as hot dogs, hamburgers, and s'mores!

Games to Get You Giggling

My game plan is always "Have fun!" When friends come over for a party or just to hang out, my favorite games get the giggles going. Try them on a party day or any day.

Camouflage

Object of the Game: To be the first to find all the objects that are hidden in plain sight.

How to Play: Someone who is not playing the game hides ten objects. The objects should be hidden in plain sight, but camouflaged by their surroundings. For example, a postage stamp hidden on the spine of a book is almost impossible to see, but it is in plain sight. Each player is given a list of the hidden items and a pencil to check off items as they are found. The first player to find them all is the winner.

Creepy Feelies

Object of the Game: To get the giggles by feeling creepy things in the dark.

How to Play: Prepare bowls of creepy things ahead of time. Peeled grapes for eyeballs; cold spaghetti for worms; dried apricots for ears; raw eggs for innards; fat pretzel sticks for bones; almonds for werewolf teeth; and a big bowl of soapy water for a "pool of acid." Turn the lights down low. Blindfold each guest. Then pass the bowls around and in a spooky voice describe what they are touching. This game will get lots of "yechs" and even more "yuks!"

Contest of Contests

Object of the Game: To win every contest.

How to Play: Each contest in the Contest of Contests is simple. All you need is a clock for timing and some willing contestants.

•**Staring Contest.** Two players stare into each other's eyes without blinking. Last to blink wins.

•**Talking Contest.** Two players start talking nonstop without pausing to think. The first to run out of things to say even for three seconds loses.

•**Handstand or Headstand Contest.** Players stand on their hands or heads. Another person times them. Last to fall wins.

•**Loudest Whistling Contest.** Players take turns whistling. Player who whistles loudest wins.

Nose Knows

Object of the Game: To correctly identify the contents of jars by scent.

How to Play: You'll need ten empty jars, ten things with different smells, and a paper and pencil for each guest. Put each thing in a different jar. Cover the outside of the jar so the contents are hidden. Number the jars. Blindfold the guests. Have guests try to identify the contents by smell alone. Players write down their guesses next to the numbers on their paper. Some things you might put in the jars are: mustard, peanut butter, vanilla, vinegar, chopped onions, perfume, tuna fish, chocolate sauce, coffee, and orange juice. The player whose nose knows the most wins.

Memory Fun

Object of the Game: To study a tray of objects and remember as many as possible.

How to Play: Someone who is not playing should set up the tray of objects. Ten to fifteen small objects (key, coin, marble, toothbrush, ring, toy car, magnet, lipstick, etc.) should be laid out on the tray. Cover the tray until playtime. Players are each given one minute to look at the tray and memorize the objects. Then the tray is covered again. Players are given five minutes to write down all of the objects they remember. The player with the most complete list wins.

Magazine Scavenger Hunt

Object of the Game: To hunt through magazines and find pictures for each letter of the alphabet from A to Z.

How to Play: Players are each given an equal number of magazines and a pad of Post-its to mark the pictures as they find them. At the word "go," players start hunting for objects for each letter of the alphabet. (For example, a picture of someone's arm for "A.") Allow 15 minutes for the hunt. The first player to find objects for the entire alphabet wins. Or, at the end of 15 minutes, the player with the most objects found wins.

Name Game

Object of the Game: To see how many words can be made from the letters in a player's name.

How to Play: Players compete to see how many words they can make out of the letters in their names. Players decide whether to use first names only, first and last names only, or first, middle, and last. The player with the longest list of words wins.

Michelle's Cool Crafts

When best friends get together, the best things happen. Doing craft projects with a friend is a great way to spend the holidays. I make all kinds of things to keep, to share, and to give as gifts. Here are just some of my most special craft ideas.

Make-Your-Own Holiday and Birthday Cards

What You'll Need: Envelopes, scissors, plain writing paper, markers.

Making cards for holidays, birthdays, or any special occasion is fun and easy. Your friends will love receiving them and you'll love making them! The only trick is figuring out what designs fit the occasion and your friend's personality best. If you know your friend loves rainbows, polka dots, or stars, choose one of those design ideas. Don't forget to use your friend's favorite color!

Fold the plain paper in half or in quarters to make a card. Use the markers to decorate each card. Decorate the envelopes to match. Write a special holiday greeting or birthday message. Then present the card to your friend. She'll be sure to treasure your work of art.

Design a Holiday T-shirt

What You'll Need: Plain T-shirts, fabric paints or markers.

The next time you and your friends get together over the weekend or holidays, have a T-shirt decorating day. Plan to make T-shirts that fit the occasion (and you!). Special Ts for Valentine's Day, Earth Day, the Fourth of July, first day of summer or somebody's birthday make great mementos of a great day!

Place plain T-shirts flat on a table covered with newspaper. Slip newspaper inside the T-shirt so the paint doesn't soak through. Use fabric markers and fabric paints to decorate. Take turns autographing one another's T-shirts. Use fancy lettering, a different color for each name, and add any designs you like. At the end of this craft project you'll each have a T-rrific souvenir.

Bubbles, Bubbles, Bubbles

What You'll Need: For bubble solution: A bowl or wide-mouthed jar, ½ cup liquid dishwashing soap, ½ cup water, ⅛ teaspoon sugar. For bubble blowers: Paper clips.

Bubbles make friends bubble over with giggles. Simply mix together the ingredients in the bubble solution recipe. Stir it until it is mixed thoroughly. To make the bubble blower, unbend a paper clip. Reshape it into a ring with a handle (like an egg dipper). Dip the ring into the bubble solution. Blow lightly. Bubbles will appear!

Holiday Hair Wear

What You'll Need: Plain plastic barrettes, headbands, clips, white glue, buttons, sequins, feathers, beads, charms, old jewelry, etc.

Barrettes and headbands don't have to be boring. A little glue and you can turn plain hair wear into holiday hair wear extraordinaire! Search your house for any items that might make good decorations. "Junk" drawers are often full of treasures. Beads from broken necklaces, old doll accessories, charms, and loose buttons are perfect craft materials. Select small items in the colors that go together well. Try out the placement of the materials first before gluing. When you have a design you like, add small amounts of glue to the hair wear. Add each item individually. Allow plenty of drying time before wearing your creations.

Make a Magic Wand

What You'll Need: Two yards of ribbon, scissors, ruler, craft glue, 24-inch long wood dowel (or stick) with ½-inch diameter, sequins, bells.

Make wishes come true for the holidays. Make your own magic wand! A simple stick decorated with streamers, bells, and sparkling sequins will do the trick when it comes to feeling magical. Cut a 24-inch piece of ribbon. Glue one end of the ribbon to one end of the wood dowel. Wrap the ribbon around the whole length of the dowel and glue it at the bottom. To add streamers, cut a few strips of ribbon. Glue one end of each strip to the top end of the dowel. Add a bell or sequin to the end of each streamer. Abracadabra, you're done!

Friendship Shoelaces

What You'll Need: Plain white or colored flat-weave shoelaces, waterproof markers.

What a perfect birthday gift to give to your best friend! Add a dash of shoelace flash to your best friend's shoes. On a paper-covered work surface, stretch out a pair of new plain shoelaces. Using your colored waterproof markers, design laces that will make your friend's shoes shine. Polka dots, curvy lines, your friend's name, hearts, flowers, candy-cane stripes, triangles, squares, or any design you choose will make a straight lace a great lace. Make a pair for a friend—and make one for yourself too!

Cheer-up Pillowcase

What You'll Need: Plain pillowcase, shirt cardboard, fabric markers.

What could be worse than being sick over the holidays? And what could be better than you showing up at the door with a Cheer-up Pillowcase gift-wrapped and ready to shoo away those home-sick blues?

When a friend is sick and tired of being sick in bed, cheer her up with this. Spread out the pillowcase and slip the cardboard inside so your markers won't soak through. Using fabric pens, design a pillowcase that is sure to bring a smile to your friend's face. Here are some happy design ideas: One big yellow smiley face or lots of little smiley faces all over the case, colorful balloons, a shower of flowers, hearts, butterflies, kites, or your friend's favorite design. Best friends do the best things for each other.

Michelle's Magic Moment
Memory Page

Now that I've shared some of my thoughts, feelings, and ideas about friendship, I hope you will too. Remember that good friends help fill holidays with good memories. Use this page to make notes about some of your best times with best friends over the holidays or any days.

_____

_____

_____

_____

_____

_____

_____

_____

_____

_____

_____

_____

Best-Friends-For-Keeps Address
and Phone List

Here's the spot to keep your list of friends'
names, phone numbers, and addresses. Be sure to
send them all holiday cards, birthday cards, and
have-a-happy-day cards.

Name: _____

Address: _____

_____

Phone: _____

Name: _____

Address: _____

_____

Phone: _____

Name: _____

Address: _____

_____

Phone: _____

Name: _____

Address: _____

_____

Phone: _____

Name: _____

Address: _____

_____

Phone: _____

82

Birthdays to Remember Not to Forget

Best friends always remember birthdays. Keep a list of your friends' and family members' birthdays here. Then remember their special days with a special card, phone call, or homemade gift from you!

Name: _____

Birthday: _____

Name: _____

Birthday: _____

Name: _____

Birthday: _____

Name: _____

Birthday: _____

Name: _____

Birthday: _____

FULL HOUSE™
Stephanie

It doesn't matter if you live around the corner...
or around the world...
If you are a fan of Mary-Kate and Ashley Olsen,
you should be a member of

MARY-KATE + ASHLEY'S FUN CLUB™

Here's what you get:
Our Funzine™
An autographed color photo
Two black & white individual photos
A full size color poster
An official **Fun Club**™ membership card
A **Fun Club**™ school folder
Two special **Fun Club**™ surprises
A holiday card
Fun Club™ collectibles catalog
Plus a **Fun Club**™ box to keep everything in

To join Mary-Kate + Ashley's Fun Club™, fill out the form
below and send it along with

U.S. Residents – $17.00
Canadian Residents – $22 U.S. Funds
International Residents – $27 U.S. Funds

MARY-KATE + ASHLEY'S FUN CLUB™
859 HOLLYWOOD WAY, SUITE 275
BURBANK, CA 91505

NAME:_____

ADDRESS:_____

_CITY:_____ STATE:_____ ZIP:_____

PHONE:(____) _____ BIRTHDATE:_____

1242

FULL HOUSE™
Michelle

#5: THE GHOST IN MY CLOSET 53573-0/$3.99

#6: BALLET SURPRISE 53574-9/$3.99

#7: MAJOR LEAGUE TROUBLE 53575-7/$3.99

#8: MY FOURTH-GRADE MESS 53576-5/$3.99

#9: BUNK 3, TEDDY, AND ME 56834-5/$3.99

**#10: MY BEST FRIEND IS A MOVIE STAR!
(Super Edition) 56835-3/$3.99**

#11: THE BIG TURKEY ESCAPE 56836-1/$3.99

#12: THE SUBSTITUTE TEACHER 00364-X/$3.99

#13: CALLING ALL PLANETS 00365-8/$3.99

#14: I'VE GOT A SECRET 00366-6/$3.99

#15: HOW TO BE COOL 00833-1/$3.99

#16: THE NOT-SO-GREAT OUTDOORS 00835-8/$3.99

#17: MY HO-HO-HORRIBLE CHRISTMAS 00836-6/$3.99

**MY AWESOME HOLIDAY FRIENDSHIP BOOK
(An Activity Book) 00840-4/$3.99**